I'M SPECIAL, TOO!

Darlene M. McCurty

African American Images

©1992

Chicago, Illinois

Cover and text illustrations by
Napoleon Wilkerson

First edition, first printing

Copyright 1992 by Darlene M. McCurty

We are God's poetry, a poem unto Him who is the true author of our lives.

 This book is dedicated to my mother, Inez. She taught my brothers, Clarence and Bruce, as well as myself, to never look down on anyone unless we are lifting them up.

Finally, to my son Rashid, who reminded me that God has given us a rainbow of gifts.

The best gift of all is to be used by God.

ACKNOWLEDGMENTS

"Train up a child in the way that he should go and when he is old he will not depart from it."

Proverbs 22:6

The Lord has blessed and showed me that nothing is impossible with faith in Him.

I would like to thank a number of people who made this book possible. They believed in me, long before I believed in myself. James W. Couch, former Suffolk County Deputy Executive, who taught me the importance of expressing myself through writing.

Florence Andresen, former Superintendent of the Glen Cove School District (and my high school literature teacher), who instructed me to always have a teachable attitude and develop my God-given gifts.

To all my friends at the Nassau County Commission on Human Rights/Job Development Center, who gave me the incentive to pursue my heart's desire.

My gratitude also goes to Deacon Cleon McCoy, who taught me how to have a true heart.

To African American Images, I thank you for opening the door and giving me the opportunity to thank Him from whom all blessings flow.

Finally, to my uncles and aunts; Leroy and William, Gloria, Oralee and Minnie, the elders of the Gibson family. You shared with me treasured memories of our ancestors and filled my heart with your words of wisdom. For these things and more, I'll continue to write with thanksgiving and love.

I'M SPECIAL, TOO!

Nehemiah Peterson was an African American boy. His skin was the color of mahogany. A dark, reddish color seemed to lie beneath his flesh. His eyes were shaped like almonds. The pupils of his eyes glowed as bright as black pearls that had just been picked from beneath the ocean. His hair was jet black, thick, and tightly-curled. It was so thick, that if it wasn't cut often, he would have a hard time combing it and it frequently looked that way. No one believed that Nehemiah was nine years old, because he was short for his age. He was repeatedly teased about his height.

Nehemiah lived in a public-housing project with his family. His father did not live with them. Nehemiah couldn't remember his father ever living with them and his mother never spoke of him. When Nehemiah was seven years old, he asked his mother where his father was. He would never forget the look she gave him. Her hypnotic gaze was like a laser beam. It was as if she was looking straight through him. Rather than show her anger, his mother chose to ignore Nehemiah's question. She knew that her expression and silence would be enough for him to ask no further questions about his father. Sensing the chill from his mother, Nehemiah realized that this was not the time to pursue the issue of his father, so he didn't push the matter any further.

When Nehemiah turned and walked away, he looked back over his shoulder at his mother. Remembering the glare in her eyes a few minutes ago, he began to fear this stranger who was sup-

1

posed to be his protector. He didn't understand what his mother was thinking about his father, but he knew it wasn't good.

He said to himself, "I'll never ask about my father again."

Nehemiah went to his room. He shared a bedroom with his five-year-old brother Zachariah, whom everyone called Zach and his sister Sarah, who was three years old. The walls in the bedroom were cracked and paint chips sometimes fell from the ceiling. Once, Sarah had to go to the hospital because she ate some paint chips that had fallen into her bed. His mother told him and Zach that Sarah had to stay in the hospital because she had lead poisoning and the doctors thought she was going to die. But after a long time, she came home. She no longer looked like his sister. Sarah's face had grown very long and thin. She had dark spots on her face, arms, and legs.

Nehemiah's mother slept in the living room on the couch. Every night, he could hear his mother talking to God and asking Him to please send her a blessing. She would cry herself to sleep and Nehemiah would also cry, even though he didn't know what a blessing was.

Sometimes there was no food for Nehemiah and Zach to eat before going to school, so their mother would give them a glass of powdered milk mixed with water.

She would say, "I did not get my check, so I could not get any food."

In the halls of their apartment building, men and women who didn't have any place to live, slept on

the steps or in a corner. The hallways always smelled like urine. On their way to school, Nehemiah and his brother saw some teenagers writing on the side of the building with spray paint. The older boys yelled and cursed at Nehemiah and Zach and began throwing rocks at them. Nehemiah grabbed his brother's hand and started running. Far from their building, they slowed down.

Zach was crying, "Nehemiah, I'm hungry and my stomach hurts."

Nehemiah answered, "You're going to have to wait until lunch time. Make sure you eat all your lunch, because we might not have a big dinner tonight."

Understanding his brother's words, Zach nodded his head while wiping his eyes with the back of his hands. By the time they arrived at school, the bell was ringing. Nehemiah saw his class going inside the building, so he hurried and took Zach to the kindergarten line-up station. Then he ran to the back of the line of his class.

All the students in Nehemiah's fourth-grade class went to the closet to hang up their coats. John Greene, a tall caucasian boy with blond hair and blue eyes, pushed Nehemiah so hard that he slipped, fell, and hit the back of his head. All of the children were laughing at him and pointing their fingers.

Some children were screaming, "Good for you, nappy head. Why don't you get a haircut?"

Their teacher, Mrs. Jones, was a short, slightly plump woman with chestnut-colored hair that was beginning to gray. Mrs. Jones rushed into the closet

3

and commanded everyone go to their seats. She bent down to help Nehemiah off the floor, but he resisted her assistance. His head was throbbing so hard, he wanted to writhe on the floor and scream loudly from the pain. But instead, he just laid still on the floor with his hands and arms wrapped around his head. Nehemiah clenched his teeth together. His eyes were tightly shut, but he still saw stars zooming back and forth in front of his face. He squeezed his lips together, so that the loud groans trying to escape his mouth remained suppressed. The last thing he wanted to do was to give John Greene and the other children another opportunity to make fun of him. Mrs. Jones was on her knees beside him.

"Let me help you off the floor," she asked softly. This time, Nehemiah didn't resist her help. He allowed Mrs. Jones to gently take his hand.

He was glad he did, because when he tried to stand, his legs were wiggling and wobbling just like jello. If it hadn't been for Mrs. Jones supporting him with her arms, he would have fallen and hit his head again. Mrs. Jones led him to a chair that was in the closet. She told him to sit down until he felt steady. He was glad of that, because if she had asked him to sit in the chair that was near his desk, he wasn't sure what he would have done.

"Barbara," Mrs. Jones called out. "Please go to the office and ask Mrs. Perry if she would come to the classroom?"

"Yes, Mrs. Jones," replied Barbara.

As Barbara scurried towards the door, Mrs. Jones continued, "And Barbara, please tell her that it is an emergency. I need her right away."

Barbara answered, "Yes, ma'am" and closed the door.

The click, clack, click, clack sounds of Barbara's shoes slipping on and off her feet were deafening. Nehemiah was familiar with the sound of shoes that were too big for one's feet, because his mother bought his shoes too big. However, he learned the secret of keeping them on his feet. He would curl his toes in the shoes until his toes got bad cramps and then he would rest them for awhile.

As Nehemiah sat in the closet, he rested his head against the coats that hung on the racks. He didn't know whose coat he was leaning on, nor did he particularly care. All he thought about was the thump, thump, thump inside his head. Mrs. Jones would not leave his side. She stood at the closet entrance, only two feet from where Nehemiah was sitting.

In a harsh tone, she faced the class and said, "I want each of you to take out your writing notebooks, copy today's topic off the board, and begin writing, now!"

Nehemiah had never heard Mrs. Jones speak so sharply. He wanted to poke his head out from the closet and say, "Ha, ha, ha" to each and every one of them.

Just then, he heard Barbara's shoes making those click, clack, click, clack sounds as she approached the classroom.

"Mrs. Jones! Mrs. Jones!" yelled Mrs. Perry nervously.

"Right here in the closet, Mrs. Perry," Mrs. Jones answered.

When Mrs. Perry saw Nehemiah she said, "Oh, my goodness! What happened, young man?" Even though he liked Mrs. Perry, who was the hall monitor, he did not feel like talking to her or answering any questions. Fortunately, he didn't have to because Mrs. Jones explained the whole thing to her. Mrs. Jones asked Mrs. Perry if she would watch the class while she took Nehemiah to the nurse's office. Mrs. Perry nodded yes and assisted Mrs. Jones in getting Nehemiah out of the chair.

When they arrived, Mrs. Candy, the nurse took Nehemiah by his arm and guided him to a chair. She looked at his head.

"You have a little bump back there, but it'll be okay," she assured him. While she was making an ice pack to put on his head, Mrs. Jones was filling her in on the details of the how the bump came about.

As Mrs. Candy listened to Mrs. Jones, she was shaking her head from side to side and asked, "When will these children ever learn how to treat others the way they would like to be treated?" Mrs. Candy, still shaking her head, walked toward Nehemiah mumbling something under her breath.

She looked at Nehemiah's head again, gave him the ice pack, and told him to hold it lightly on the bump. She patted his shoulder gently, smiled at him and walked back over to her desk and began filling

out some papers. Mrs. Jones asked Nehemiah if he felt any better. He shook his head to answer yes, but instantly wished he had used his mouth to answer instead. His head felt like a stampede of wild horses were running through his brain. Nehemiah grimaced in pain. Mrs. Jones saw his discomfort and told him to return to class only if he felt better.

When Nehemiah arrived back in class, Mrs. Jones was lecturing the students. She was telling them about the class rule which states, "NO FIGHT-ING". She continued by telling them that their class-room was their home away from home and everyone should try to be one big, happy family. Mrs. Jones then focused her attention toward Nehemiah.

"How are you feeling, Nehemiah?" she asked.

"Much better," he answered in almost a whisper.

"The class has something to say to you," she announced.

In unison they said, "We're sorry."

Nehemiah didn't want to look at them, so he stared at the floor and just moved his head slightly. Nehemiah took his seat in the third row which faced a large window. He loved to look out of the window and watch the birds glide and soar across the sky. Sometimes, birds would land on the ledge of the window and start chirping, as if they were talking to each other. Nehemiah would pretend he was talking to the birds and only they could hear or understand him. He enjoyed this and looked for-ward to this time with his friends. Today, he was telling the birds about the incident with John

Greene. He also told them how the children were calling him names and making fun of him.

Nehemiah did not have breakfast before leaving home that morning. He was just about to tell the birds how hungry he was, when he heard Mrs. Jones calling his name, "Nehemiah! You must pay attention in class and please stop daydreaming!"

All the children began snickering at him.

Mrs. Jones announced, "Today class, you will have a spelling quiz."

Sighs could be heard throughout the room. Nehemiah knew that he was going to have trouble. Even if he told Mrs. Jones that his head was beginning to hurt again, which it wasn't, when he took the test, the results would still be the same: not good.

For some reason when he wrote, his words always looked right to him, but he could hear Mrs. Jones saying, "Nehemiah, the word 'baby' begins with a 'b' not a 'd'."

Or she would say, "The word 'pack' is written like this and not 'qack'."

Nehemiah remembered once when they had a spelling bee, everyone had to be divided into teams and none of the children wanted him to be on their team. Mrs. Jones told him that he would be on the blue team. Mary Johnson was the captain of that team. She was also caucasian, just like John Greene. She had very long red hair. When she walked or shook her head to answer no, her hair would bounce wildly. Mary's face was the color of chalk. She had red freckles on her nose and cheeks. She

8

was very smart and everyone always wanted to be her friend.

Mary started yelling, "Why does he have to be on my team? He can't spell. He can't read. He's a space cadet!"

The children all began laughing hysterically, some even made funny faces at him.

John Greene put his thumbs in his ears, contorted his face, and started saying, "Space cadet, space cadet."

The other children joined in. Nehemiah wanted to become invisible. No one in his class liked him.

Mrs. Jones took the ruler from her desk drawer and hit it against the edge of the desk yelling, "Stop this, right now!"

When she wasn't looking, they continued making faces at him. Today's quiz would be no different. Now he wished he had left school when Mrs. Candy offered to drive him home, after hitting his head.

Propping his chin on his fist, Nehemiah thought to himself, "I can certainly tell that this day is not going to be one of my better days."

Then he thought again, "There's no such thing as a better day for me," and he let out a deep sigh.

Mrs. Jones stood in front of the classroom and began pronouncing the words for the spelling test. "The word for number one is..." She continued in this manner for all ten of the words.

After she finished, she asked everyone to pass their papers to the front of the room. At the same time the children were passing their papers, Mr. Mack, the art teacher came into the classroom to

give them their art lesson. Mrs. Jones embarked on correcting the spelling tests. Mrs. Jones called Nehemiah to her desk and asked him to see her after school. He knew it was about the spelling test.

Nehemiah went back to his seat and stared out of the window. He watched the clouds float across the sky. He wished he was a cloud. The life of a cloud seemed so carefree. They were never hungry because God always made sure they had rain to drink. He knew that sometimes clouds got angry with each other and when they were fighting or arguing, he would hear thunder and see lightning travel across the sky. Nehemiah continued getting lost in his thoughts. When one of his bird friends came back on the ledge, he started smiling. The little bird began chirping away.

"Oh, how I wish I could spread my arms and fly," thought Nehemiah. "I would fly so high and the sun would soothe me with its warmth. I wouldn't have to worry about getting thirsty, because I would drink the raindrops and wash my body squeaky clean in the droplets. I would eat from any tree in the world and never again would I be hungry."

Once again, Mrs. Jones interrupted his daydreams, "Nehemiah! I'm not going to tolerate your daydreaming any longer. I want you to remain after school today!"

Nehemiah was so startled that he jumped. He forgot that he was in school. He didn't even remember when the art teacher left. He looked at the clock and it was lunch time. The children gathered their lunch boxes and proceeded to the lunchroom.

After lunch was over, they were back in their classroom and Mrs. Jones had a guest speaker waiting for them. His name was Mr. Gross. He was an airplane pilot. He wore a uniform and a hat. He even had a pin on his jacket that was shaped like bird wings. Nehemiah was mesmerized by what Mr. Gross had to say. He was staring at Mr. Gross as if he were in a trance, thinking about the bird wings that he was wearing on his jacket. Nehemiah didn't even hear Mr. Gross say that he was finished. The children all clapped and thanked Mr. Gross for coming.

The dismissal bell was ringing. It was time for everyone to go home. Everyone except Nehemiah. Mrs. Jones called each row to get their coats and book bags. When all the children were in line to go home, some of them were pointing their fingers at Nehemiah and giggling. Nehemiah folded his arms on the desk and put his head in his arms, hoping Mrs. Jones would hurry up and dismiss the class.

When Mrs. Jones returned to class, she closed the door. Nehemiah's heart began to beat fast and loud. It was beating so loud that he could feel it in his throat. He even thought Mrs. Jones heard it. She pulled up a chair and sat down next to him. "How does your head feel," she asked?

"Much better, ma'am," he stuttered.

Nehemiah nearly forgot about the bump on his head. When he felt his head during lunch, the bump had almost disappeared. All he could think about now was the test that he knew he failed. Sure enough, when Mrs. Jones opened the folder she had been carrying, he saw the only paper that looked like graffiti.

"Nehemiah," she began. "I think we have a problem. You failed your test today."

Nehemiah looked at the test that Mrs. Jones was holding. It appeared correct to him. Mrs. Jones explained that his 'b' should have been a 'd' and his 'd' should have been a 'b'. Mrs. Jones pointed to the word 'was'.

Nehemiah said to himself, "I spelled that word right! Why did she mark it wrong?"

Mrs. Jones said, "W-a-s- spells 'was.' The word that I gave you was 'saw', spelled s-a-w-."

Nehemiah looked hard at the way he spelled the word 'was' and the way Mrs. Jones spelled 'saw'. It looked the same to him. However, he did not say anything to Mrs. Jones because she might get angry with him. He just apologized and promised to do better next time.

"Nehemiah," Mrs. Jones asked, "how do you expect to get promoted to the fifth grade, if all you do is daydream?" She continued, "Don't you realize that I'm here for you? I don't want to just be your teacher, I also want to be your friend. If something is bothering you, please come and let me know or write me a letter and leave it on my desk. I promise you, we will work it out together."

Nehemiah looked into Mrs. Jones eyes while she was talking. They were saying to him that she meant every word she said. He believed she really wanted to help him and be his friend. He needed a friend. There was no one he could call his friend, except Zach or Sarah. But they didn't count as friends, they were his brother and sister.

Nehemiah asked Mrs. Jones if he could stay a few minutes longer because he wanted to copy the work from the board that he missed earlier that afternoon. She gave him permission to remain until she left. He knew he wasn't going to copy just the assignment from the board. He had to talk to someone and Mrs. Jones was the only person who had ever said she wanted to be his friend. He could never talk to his mother, especially after he asked her about his father. She gave him a look that he would never forget. He didn't want to risk that happening again. Anyway, Mrs. Jones did say he could write her a letter and leave it on her desk. So he began to write.

"Dear Mrs. Jones, I don't know why I can't do anything right. Every day, I try real hard to get things right, but it's always wrong. When I take a test, it seems right to me. But when I get my test back, there are always red marks on my paper and a great big red 'F', which means that I got a zero. Sometimes when I think that I know the work, you always show me that I don't understand at all. I am going to do better because I want you to be my friend. You are the only friend I have. No one in the class likes me. They call me names and talk about my clothes. The reason I daydream is because it's the only place that I fit in. It's my world, a place where I can do everything right, even spelling. In my world, I can talk to birds and they talk to me. I wish people were as friendly to me as animals are." Nehemiah continued writing, "Mrs. Jones, do you think maybe God made a mistake when he made me a person? Maybe I'm supposed to be a bird or another kind of animal. That would explain why they like me and people hate me. Once, my mother told me that I was a mistake. Parents are always right, aren't they? You can write me back if you want. Your friend, Nehemiah."

Nehemiah folded the letter. How could he put it on Mrs. Jones' desk without her noticing? He slowly held his head up and peeked to see what Mrs. Jones was doing. She was busy writing something in her book. Then she got up from her desk and told Nehemiah that she had to go to the office and would be right back. Nehemiah watched as Mrs. Jones went down the hall. When he was out of sight, he quickly got his coat and book bag from the closet. He dropped the letter on the book that Mrs. Jones had been writing in and ran out of the door without putting on his coat.

Nehemiah jumped down the four steps that led outside. He stumbled, but did not get hurt. The book bag opened and his books, papers, and coat landed in the dirt. He immediately brushed his clothes off and shook the dirt off his coat and book bag while peeking around to see if anyone saw him.

Just then, he heard a small voice laughing, "Ah-ha Nehemiah, I saw you. I saw you."

Nehemiah recognized the well-known laughter. It was his brother, Zach. Zach knew never to walk home alone or to leave with anyone other than Nehemiah. Whenever Nehemiah was too ill to attend school, his mother kept Zach home also. She would complain of arthritis in her legs and was unable to walk Zach to school. However, Zach didn't mind waiting after school for Nehemiah. He waited for him at the playground, where there were sliding boards, swings, and jungle gyms. He was never there alone. Other children were also waiting there to be picked up. Mrs. Perry always stayed in the playground until every child had left. Zach made friends easily and the children liked him. He was the most popular student in his class. He was just the opposite of his brother.

The next day, when Nehemiah returned to school, he wondered if Mrs. Jones would embarrass him and read his letter to the class. He knew if she did, that he would die right there on the spot!

When all the children were seated, Mrs. Jones said, "Everyone take out your writing notebooks."

Nehemiah looked dumbfounded and thought, "Maybe someone else came in here and took the letter from her desk. Oh no!" Nehemiah gasped loudly and everyone stared at him. Mrs. Jones asked him if anything was wrong.

"I'm very sorry," Nehemiah replied.

Mrs. Jones announced, "Today class, we have a creative writing project. The school district will choose the best writing assignment from the fourth-grade class and enter it in the Statewide Creative Writing Contest."

John Bono, an Italian boy said, "I know Nehemiah isn't going to be chosen. His writing always says 'duh, duh duh'."

The children all roared with laughter. But Nehemiah was so accustomed to ridicule, that he said nothing. Mrs. Jones told the class that if there were any more outbursts like that again, she would call the parents of every student involved. The class suddenly became so quiet that if a feather fell, you would be able to hear it.

Nehemiah once thought the reason the children didn't like him and picked on him all the time was because he was the only African American student in the class. But he knew that wasn't the reason because he came back to school after summer vacation, opened the door to his class and there sat the most beautiful girl he had ever seen in his life. Her name was Deirdre Horton.

She was an African American girl whose complexion was the shade of caramel candy. Her two long braids that hung down the side of her face had red ribbons on the end of them which seemed to make her face blush. She looked at Nehemiah and smiled. What did she do that for! His heart began doing somersaults, flipping and flopping inside his chest.

Nehemiah remembered how friendly she was. All of the students liked her. John Greene was always asking her if he could sharpen her pencils. Whenever they had a spelling bee, Mary Johnson would pick Deirdre first, because she got good grades on her tests the way Mary did.

Deirdre tried to be friends with Nehemiah. Whenever she attempted to talk to him, he would freeze and say nothing. He was afraid that if he said too many words to her, she would see how dumb he was and begin laughing at him like the other children. But every morning he came to school, she said, "Good morning, Nehemiah."

He thought if he said anything more than that, his tongue would get tangled and he would trip over his words. Nehemiah continued reflecting, "March 16th. I'll never forget that day, when I opened the classroom door expecting to see Deirdre, but she was nowhere to be found."

Nehemiah remembered Mrs. Jones announcing that Deirdre would not be coming back to school, because her family had moved to California. A lot of the students were sad, especially John Greene. Nehemiah felt abandoned. Even though he never said much to her, he looked forward to seeing her everyday.

He missed hearing her say, "Good morning, Nehemiah," in her bubbly and excited voice.

She had been the only person in the class that spoke and smiled at him everyday. How he wished he had been able to hold a real conversation with her. But now it was too late. He knew he would never see her again. Ever. He missed her very, very much.

The loud sound of Mrs. Jones clapping her hands together and speaking in a high-pitched voice saying, "Children, children, give me your attention now," brought him back to the present. Mrs. Jones continued, "Now that I have your attention, every student in this class will participate in the Statewide Creative Writing Contest. The topic that you will write about is 'If I Could Be Anything/ Or Anyone In The World, I'd Like To Be...'" Mrs. Jones proceeded, "You will explain in full detail, why you would like to be the thing or person you chose."

proceeded, "You will explain in full detail, why you would like to be the thing or person you chose."

Everyone started mumbling under their breath. Mrs. Jones asked if anyone had any questions. No one said anything. Mrs. Jones wrote the topic on the board.

John Greene raised his hand and commented, "Can I say that I'd like to be a cyclops?"

Laughter from the class could be heard down the corridor. Everyone was laughing, including Mrs. Jones. No one heard Mr. Smith, the principal, come in.

"Good morning boys and girls," he said. "By now, your teacher should have explained to you about the Statewide Creative Writing Contest." He continued, "Creative writing is when you use your imagination and daydreams, give your thoughts life, and make them become real on paper. I hope one of the selected essays to enter the contest comes from the fourth-grade class here at Garvey Elementary School." With his arm stretched toward the ceiling and his fist clenched, he yelled in a loud voice, "Now give it all you have! I know that you can do it, boys and girls."

Some of the children extended their arms in the same manner as Mr. Smith.

The other children hollered, clapped their hands and cheered, "Yeah, yeah, yeah."

For a moment, the classroom sounded like an after school basketball game. But Mr. Smith quickly calmed the class down and wished everyone good luck. He told everyone to do their very best, then he left.

The only word that Nehemiah focused on was the word daydreams. Mrs. Jones had always interrupted him when he was daydreaming. Now, they wanted the class to write about daydreams. Nehemiah took out his notebook and pencil. He started to stare out of the window. The clouds seemed to roll by slowly and wink at him. The birds that flew by the window waved their feathery arms in his direction, as if they were wishing him good luck. Nehemiah began to write.

"If I could be anything in the world, I'd like to be a bird. Birds always seem to have other birds with them when they fly. They never seem to be alone. When they are hungry, there is always food for them to eat. When they get thirsty, they drink rain water or water from the lakes. Birds do not have to wait for their mothers to get a check so that they can eat. They sleep in nests that are high in the trees. When it's real cold outside, they fly south where it is warm and live there. They do not have mice in their homes, holes in their walls, or even paint chips falling from their ceilings. They play in the sky with their friends and have fun. Life for birds is great. I really wish I was a bird. I wish my mother, brother, and sister were birds too. Then, my mother would not cry all the time and ask God for a blessing. My brother Zach wouldn't have to cry all night because there wasn't enough food for dinner to fill him up and my sister Sarah would never have to stay in the hospital again because she ate pieces of paint chips that fell from the ceiling. If I were a bird, I would fly all around the world. I would ask my other bird friends to help me find my

NAPOLEON WILKERSON 92.

father. When I found him, I'd tell him how much I miss him and love him. I would ask him to please come home. I'd promise to be a good boy and I'd make Zach and Sarah be good too. I know if my father were home, I wouldn't have to wish I were a bird. Then I could be a person and he would take care of me. He would also take me for haircuts and buy me new clothes and shoes. This is why if I could be anything in the world, I'd choose to be a bird."

Nehemiah was deep in thought. He didn't even hear the lunch bell ring. Mrs. Jones had to tap him on the shoulder to get his attention.

She spoke very softly and asked, "Nehemiah, would you like to share my lunch with me today?"

Nehemiah replied, "Yes, ma'am."

After the children headed for the lunch room, Nehemiah and Mrs. Jones sat in the back of the room at the large reading table.

Mrs. Jones said, "I hope you like chicken salad sandwiches." Chicken was Nehemiah's favorite food. Nehemiah didn't say much during lunch. Mrs. Jones did most of the talking.

When she would ask him a question, he would reply, "Yes, ma'am" or "No, ma'am".

Nothing more. Observing his uneasiness, Mrs. Jones ate the remainder of her lunch silently. She smiled at Nehemiah every now and then, hoping that he would relax enough so that his food could digest properly. He ate the last bite of his sandwich, trying to make as little noise as possible while chewing. He didn't want Mrs. Jones to think that he was a pig. He finished his milk and wiped his mouth with the napkin Mrs. Jones gave him. "Thank you, Mrs. Jones," he stated.

He was just about to ask if he could be excused, when Mrs. Jones informed him that she read the letter he left on her desk yesterday. She said that she was glad they were friends.

She informed him, "I spoke with Mrs. Martin, the resource room teacher. She helps students like you who have problems with seeing certain letters and words backwards." Mrs. Jones assured Nehemiah that Mrs. Martin was a very nice teacher and she would help him see letters and words the way everyone else sees them.

Nehemiah was so happy that Mrs. Jones was his friend and that she cared so much about him. Mrs. Jones made arrangements for him to be in Mrs. Martin's class everyday during the third period. Nehemiah looked at Mrs. Jones. He wanted to throw his arms around her and tell her how much he appreciated what she did for him, but he dared not. He just looked at Mrs. Jones whose white teeth were sparkling so bright, that they made his eyes glare. She was smiling at him and he smiled back.

"Thank you, Mrs. Jones," he said.

The children were returning to class from lunch. Mrs. Jones announced that everyone had to finish their essay today and she would get together later this evening with the judges of the contest to read them over.

The children settled down at their desks. They were all eager to continue with their writing assignment. Every student seemed to be off on his/her different adventures and exploring as they went

along. Mrs. Jones observed the children from her desk. Never had she seen the children take to an assignment with such vigor. Even John Greene who usually interrupted the class periodically, because he had to be the class clown, was busy working and smiling at his thoughts while he wrote.

Mary Johnson sat extremely straight in her chair while she was writing. Her posture appeared to say, "This is so easy for me. I know I'm going to write the best paper, because I'm the smartest person in this class. I bet I'm the smartest person in this whole school! Everyone likes me."

Mrs. Jones' eyes searched the third row. Nehemiah was gazing hypnotically out of the window. His eyes were tilted up toward the sky. He seemed to be riding on the gentle breeze that was moving outside through the air. Mrs. Jones did not even entertain the thought of bringing him back to reality. He looked so contented, so at peace with himself. It was as if he was one with the universe. Mrs. Jones busied herself with grading papers.

Before Mrs. Jones realized it, the afternoon had flown by quickly. The children handed in their writing assignments and gathered their coats and book bags and were ready for dismissal.

As Nehemiah walked home, he thought about what he had written in class.

He said to himself, "Maybe I shouldn't have written about being a bird. Mrs. Jones might start calling me a space cadet, the way John Greene and the other children did. Oh, why did I write that I wanted to be a bird?"

Nehemiah felt as if everyone who was walking home looked at him and knew that he wanted to be a bird. He wished the earth would open large enough to swallow him in one big gulp. No one would miss him. They would see the earth open up its mouth to eat him and they would keep on walking home.

When Nehemiah walked up the four flights of stairs to his apartment, he didn't even cover his nose or quickly run up the stairs. He often did this to avoid the stench of urine or the different aromas of food being cooked that came through the doors of the apartments. Today, he was thinking about the paper he wrote and wondered if Mrs. Jones would still be his friend after she read it. He was thinking about the paper so much, that he didn't realize he had walked up an extra flight of stairs and was now on the fifth floor. He went down one flight, to apartment 4-D where he lived and knocked on the door. When his mother opened the door, he didn't smell anything cooking and today he didn't even care. Nehemiah's mother wasn't dressed. She had the same night clothes on that she was wearing this morning. Her hair was sticking all over her head. It looked as if she had stuck her hand in an electrical socket. The television was on and she yelled to Nehemiah to hurry up, come in, and close the door because he was making her miss her story. His mother ran, jumped on the couch, and tucked her legs and feet underneath her. She propped her chin in her hand.

Before Nehemiah could close the front door, he heard his mother bellow, "Now see what you did! I don't know if Jake was saved or not! Now I'll have to wait until tomorrow."

Nehemiah walked rapidly through the tiny living room, where his mother was watching television and opened the door to his bedroom. Zach was lying on the floor doing his homework. Today, he didn't have to wait and come home with Nehemiah. His class had a half-day because his teacher had a meeting with all of the parents to let them know how their children were doing in school. Zach knew his mother wasn't going to come. She never came to school for anything. This often bothered him and he would cry. Eventually, it didn't matter anymore. Sometimes, he wouldn't even show her the happy faces that his teacher put on his papers. He would show Nehemiah and then fold them neatly and hide them in a box in his closet.

Today, Mrs. Gonzales, a Spanish woman who also spoke English and lived in the apartment directly underneath theirs, brought him home along with her daughter Sonya. His mother never visited Mrs. Gonzales unless Zach's class had a half-day.

She would say, "Mrs. Gonzales, my arthritis is acting up today and I can't move my legs that much,"

Or she would say,"I've been dizzy all day. Would you mind picking up Zach for me?"

Mrs. Gonzales was very nice. She always said yes. Once she gave his mother some medicine for her arthritis. But when she went home, she threw the medicine in the garbage.

Sarah was in a corner by the window, talking and playing with her doll. Nehemiah playfully rubbed Zach on the head and kissed Sarah on her cheek.

Zach said, "Look at my gold star the teacher gave me. I got all my work right and Mrs. Brown said my work was great." Zach was smiling so proudly, he looked like the President did on television last night.

Nehemiah told his brother that he was smart. He loved his brother and sister and they loved him. He always defended them when their mother would tell them that she was going to spank them if they didn't be quiet so she could hear the television. Nehemiah would immediately respond and let his mother know that he was the one responsible for them making so much noise and wouldn't do it again.

Nehemiah's mother opened the door to their room and told them to come and eat. Zach jumped up off the floor and was the first one to sit at the table. Nehemiah lifted Sarah into a chair and sat down next to her. He still couldn't smell any food that had been cooking, nor were there any pots on the stove. His mother put a sandwich that was cut in half in front of Zach, and gave him and Sarah the same thing. She then took the box of powdered milk from the cabinet, mixed it with water, and put a little sugar in it.

Nehemiah thought, "When I grow up, I'm never going to drink powdered milk again! And I'm never giving it to my children."

When Nehemiah lifted the bread to see what was between the slices, he saw it was cheese. He did not like cheese, but he didn't let his mother know.

She put a glass of milk in front of each of them and said, "Make sure you eat everything and drink all of your milk, it's very good for you."

Nehemiah wasn't interested in the food in front of him. He kept thinking that tomorrow he had to face Mrs. Jones. He knew she would probably be waiting for him in front of the school building. Nehemiah's head began to hurt. He swallowed the last drop of milk and went to his room. He laid across the bed. He couldn't concentrate on anything except that writing assignment that he did in school today.

"Why did I write that I wished I was a bird?" Nehemiah whined out loud.

He was thinking about school. His mother opened the door to his room and told him to bathe and go to bed. Later that night when everyone was in bed, Nehemiah could not fall asleep. He tossed and turned and kicked off the cover.

He was dreaming that when he opened the door to his classroom, the children all yelled out, "Here comes Nehemiah, the bird boy. Take a seat, birdbrain."

Everyone was laughing hysterically. Even Mrs. Jones laughed at him.

Mrs. Jones said, "Let's all do the bird dance."

Mrs. Jones, along with the entire class, all began to run around the classroom making chirping sounds and flapping their arms wildly. Nehemiah tried to push his way out of the classroom, but the more he persisted, the wilder everyone became. He awoke from his dream drenched in sweat. He sat up and stared out of the window in his bedroom.

It was raining hard and the drops of rain that hit the fire escape seemed to tell him, "Everything is going to be alright, don't worry."

Nehemiah slowly lowered his body back down in his bed. He put his hands behind his head and continued listening to the sounds of the heavy rain hitting the fire escape. Before he knew it, he had fallen asleep. He was sleeping so soundly, that he didn't hear his mother telling him and Zach to get up and get ready for school.

Zach came over to his bed and shook him. "Nehemiah, get up," he said.

Nehemiah sleepily looked out the window and noticed that the rain had stopped. He jumped out of bed and went to the bathroom to brush his teeth and wash his face. He got dressed, ate his oatmeal, drank his milk, and left for school with Zach. When they got to the first floor in the building, an old man was lying on the floor in a corner with a raggedy blanket covering him. He smelled as if he had never taken a bath in his life. The old man had no teeth in his mouth. When he saw the two boys, he asked them for a quarter. Nehemiah shook his head no and kept walking. Zach just stared blankly at the old man and didn't say a word.

While they were walking to school, Zach talked nonstop. But Nehemiah was not paying attention to him today. His mind was on the dream that he had last night. He tried to shake the thought from his head and think about something else, but the dream kept coming back. When they were near the school, Nehemiah saw John Greene on the other side of the street walking with some older boys. Nehemiah turned his head quickly, hoping that John Greene wouldn't see him and start calling him names. Nehemiah grabbed Zach's hand and quickened his pace, so he wouldn't have to arrive at school the same time as John Greene and his friends.

Nehemiah was the first to get in line this morning.

He hurried into the classroom, put his things away, and took his seat. Mary Johnson walked by and stuck her tongue out at him. She tilted her head up in the air and grunted as she walked past. Mrs. Jones asked everyone to take their seats. All the students quickly sat down at their desks and waited to hear if one of their essays had been selected to enter the contest. Mrs. Jones couldn't believe that she didn't have to ask the students twice to take their seats. They were all sitting quietly with their hands folded on their desks.

Mrs. Jones began, "The judges and I read your essays last night. Never have I seen such a group of talented young writers. However, difficult as it was for us to choose only one essay, I am proud to say that the paper that has been selected to enter the Statewide Creative Writing Contest belongs to Nehemiah Peterson."

The silence that earlier enveloped the class, suddenly became sounds of hissing and buzzing.

Nehemiah said to himself, "This must be a joke that Mrs. Jones is playing on me. I know she's about to yell, 'April fool, bird boy!' even though this isn't April."

Nehemiah looked around the room, all eyes were on him. Mary Johnson had stretched her eyes and her mouth opened so wide, that it looked as if she was waiting for a doctor to tell her to say 'ah'.

John Greene was slapping the sides of his head and repeating loudly, "I don't believe it! I don't believe it!"

Mrs. Jones asked everyone to quiet down. She then asked Nehemiah to stand up. Slowly he got out of his chair and leaned against the desk. He was afraid of falling flat on his face. Nehemiah's heart was beating fast and his body was trembling.

"I'm going to be sick," he thought. But just as he was thinking about being sick, Mr. Smith came into the classroom and stood near Mrs. Jones. She handed him a paper. Nehemiah knew it was his.

Mr. Smith said, "Nehemiah, I'm proud of you, young man. And everyone here at Garvey Elementary School is proud of you, too."

Nehemiah looked around at the astonished faces of his classmates.

"Proud? No. Stunned is more like it," he speculated.

Mr. Smith continued, "Last night, when the judges read through hundreds of papers for the contest, yours was one that had that extra something."

Nehemiah tried to listen to Mr. Smith, but said to himself, "This must be another dream. Or maybe they have me mixed up with another Nehemiah Peterson."

Mr. Smith cleared his throat. "Let me say again, Nehemiah, that Mrs. Jones and I are delighted that your essay was selected to enter the Statewide Creative Writing Contest."

Mrs. Jones stood smiling broadly. Nehemiah thought he could see every tooth in her mouth. Mr. Smith asked all of the students to give Nehemiah a round of applause. There was hesitation from the class, but when Mr. Smith and Mrs. Jones started clapping, they joined in.

Mary raised her hand and in a quivering but loud voice, she stated, "I believe that a mistake has been made, Mr. Smith. I wrote a superb essay, just like all of the other assignments that I've done in this class. I have ALWAYS received the highest grade."

She looked around the room to make sure that her friends confirmed what she was saying. Satisfied with their alliance, she returned her attention to Mr. Smith and Mrs. Jones, hoping to get the same reaction from them. But they didn't say anything. Unconcerned, Mary kept talking.

"I went home last night and recited my entire essay to my parents. I'm smart like my father, you know," she boasted. "When they heard my essay," Mary's voice began to get louder and shakier, "they told me that I definitely had the winning essay, because I'M SMART! I was born smart. My parents always told me how I learned everything faster than all of their friends' children or my cousins. And they told me that I was EXTRA SPECIAL."

Mary looked at Nehemiah and rolled her eyes.

"Mr. Smith and Mrs. Jones, I truly believe that if you and the judges will recheck the essays and read mine first, you will see that a big mistake has been made. My paper should have been the one that was selected from this district to enter into the Statewide Creative Writing Contest. Definitely not Nehemiah Peterson's essay."

She pounded her fist against the desk and tossed her fiery, red hair which was now the same color as her face. She sat down so forcefully, that one of the stationary guards on the leg of the chair popped off.

The facial expressions of both Mr. Smith and Mrs. Jones showed how angry they were with Mary. Mrs. Jones was the first to speak.

In a very stern voice, she told Mary, "Every student in this class does great work!" She went on to say, "Being smart does not mean getting one hundred on your papers all the time and then thumbing your nose at those who didn't get one hundred.

A truly smart person is one who offers to help others without being asked. A truly smart person is one who does not look down on someone just because that person may be less fortunate. A smart person is one who extends a helping hand because she never knows when she may need help."

Mr. Smith shook his head in agreement with everything Mrs. Jones was saying.

"I couldn't have explained it better, Mrs. Jones," he stated. "The selection remains as it is!"

Mary sat in her chair quietly. She didn't look around the room as she usually did to see who was on her side. Instead, she stared at the two adults in front of the class. Mary was numb. No one, not even her parents, had ever spoken to her with such sternness. She didn't know if she was angry at Mrs. Jones or not. Maybe Mrs. Jones saw something about her that wasn't nice. Maybe she was telling her that she wasn't as smart as she thought she was. But Mary knew one thing for sure, Mrs. Jones words were going through her mind like an echo in a cave. Those words kept vibrating its message against the walls of her brain and then piercing her ears again and again.

In a low voice, Mary uttered to herself, "Could I have possibly been wrong?"

Nehemiah had sat back down in his seat when Mary first began to rant and rave. The entire class was sitting quietly with their hands folded on their desks. Mrs. Jones looked around and for a moment thought she was standing in front of her Bible school students.

Mr. Smith informed the students, "Over the coming weekend, the Governor of the State and his panel of judges will select one winner in the Statewide Creative Writing Contest. They will then inform all the principals of the schools and I will then make the announcement over the loudspeaker."

Mr. Smith smiled, then left the classroom.

Nehemiah still could not believe that his paper had been selected. He pinched his arms.

"Ouch," he winced and said, "Maybe I am still dreaming." He closed his eyes, only to open them again to the same classroom. The children were already settled and began copying their assignment from the board. Mrs. Jones didn't even have to tell anyone to stop talking, get to work, or behave themselves. Little did she know, that they were all quietly doing some soul searching and wondering, "Have I ever done any of those things that Mrs. Jones says a truly smart person does?"

It was so quiet in the classroom, Mrs. Jones stopped writing in her plan book, looked up and softly whispered, "Peace be still." She continued, "Peace, in here you have found a quiet place to slumber. Rest and allow us to enjoy your tranquility, even if it is only for a short while."

Nehemiah was totally lost in his thoughts. He didn't realize that this was the third period. Mrs. Martin, the resource room teacher, was there to escort him back to her classroom. Mrs. Martin had helped Nehemiah tremendously with his letters and words. She told him that the name of his problem was called dyslexia. She said that a lot of children and adults sometimes read things backwards and she would help him remedy his problem. And she did. Nowadays when he wrote, he rarely made his 'b' look like 'd'. Even Mrs. Jones said he had made excellent progress.

Today, as Nehemiah walked down the hall along with Mrs. Martin, teachers were congratulating him on winning the contest. He didn't realize that so many people knew who he was. No one did before. He saw several of Zach's classmates waiting in front of the nurse's office to get their eyes tested.

When Sonya, the little Spanish girl who lives in the apartment underneath his saw him, she whispered in a loud voice, "That's Zachariah's brother. He's the fourth-grader that our teacher said won that contest."

Nehemiah turned his head in their direction. All of them started giggling. He thought Zach was there in line, but he wasn't.

As Nehemiah and Mrs. Martin continued down the long hall, she was telling him she felt honored that one of her students had been selected to be one of the finalists. She told him that she would keep her fingers crossed for him until the winner was selected next Monday.

When school had ended, Nehemiah was getting ready to get Zach, but remembered that today was an early dismissal for him. He went home with Mrs. Gonzales and Sonya. Nehemiah walked home with his head up. Today, he didn't feel like looking at the ground, asking the earth to swallow him up. No, today he felt special.

He even said out loud, "I feel special today."

However, he only said it loud enough so that he could hear it. As Nehemiah was talking to himself, he thought he heard someone calling his name. He stopped and looked around, only to see John Greene and his friend running towards him.

"Hey Nehemiah, wait up," they yelled. Nehemiah's heart skipped a beat.

He wondered, "Why do they want to pick on me today of all days?"

Before they caught up to him, Nehemiah said to himself, "I'm not going to let them get the best of me. My essay was selected fair and square. Those were my daydreams that I wrote about. I didn't

copy them from anyone and they can't take it from me."

When John Greene and his friend were standing next to Nehemiah, they all wanted to know what his essay was about. "About birds," he uttered.

"How can anybody write about birds and win a contest?" asked one of the older boys. "Birds are dumb. They don't do anything but fly. Once, I almost hit a bird with my slingshot, but I missed and he flew away." Some of the boys were laughing.

However, John Greene remembered what Mrs. Jones said, "If you look down on others, then one day people will look down on you."

In a voice that everyone could hear, he said, "I rather like birds myself."

No one said a word. John Greene began to walk away and the other boys followed him. As Nehemiah turned and continued to walk home, he thought about what just happened. It wasn't what John Greene said, it was the way he said it. It sounded somewhat--friendly. Nehemiah, finding it hard to believe what just happened, turned to look at the departing boys.

Nehemiah felt as if he was walking on air. His feet were on a magic carpet, gliding him to the entrance of his apartment building. He put his hand over his nose and ran up the stairs to his floor. When he reached his apartment, he took his hand away from his nose. He thought he smelled fried chicken coming from his apartment. Nehemiah knocked on the door. When his mother opened the door, the aroma and the sound of chicken frying greeted him. The television was even turned off!

The only talking he heard was coming from the kitchen, where Mr. Chicken Wing and Mr. Drumstick were holding a loud conversation and having a popping good time in the frying pan.

Nehemiah did a double take when he realized that the person who opened the door was his mother. Her hair was combed nicely and she wore a dress that was so blue, she could have been part of the sky. She looked at Nehemiah and smiled. Then she grabbed him and squeezed him so tight, he could barely breathe.

Nehemiah wondered what was going on. Why was his mother cooking his favorite food? Why was her hair fixed nicely? And, why was she dressed up?

Before he could ask anything, she said, "Nehemiah, do you remember when I went on a job interview at the post office a few months ago?"

Nehemiah nodded yes.

She continued excitedly, "Well, this morning they called and asked me if I was still interested in the job! I told them of course I was still interested." Her voice quickened, "To make a long story short, they asked me to come and get my personnel information. I did, the job is mine and I start in two weeks!" she shrieked.

Nehemiah had never seen his mother so happy. She was behaving just like a little girl who worked hard for the lead part in a play and finally got it. He didn't know how to respond.

"Nehemiah," his mother said in a saddened voice. "I know that I haven't been the best mother. I've been feeling sorry for myself and thinking only about how miserable my life is. I didn't have anything to really look forward to." She continued, "Even when I went on the interview at the post office. After I didn't hear from them in a few weeks, I assumed they found someone else for the position. But when the phone rang this morning...Anyway, now I feel like our future is not so bleak. We might even be able to move from this apartment soon." She was smiling hopefully at him. "Nehemiah," she went on, "parents don't always have the right ingredients to be good parents. Even though we are adults and our children think we should know all of the answers, that's not the case. We learn day by day as we go through life, just the way children do. The only way anyone gets better at anything is through practice." She continued. "What I'm saying Nehemiah, is that I know I haven't been a very good mother, but I intend on working hard at it everyday from now on. My grandmother said if you prayed faithfully with a true heart, the Lord would always answer. She was right." Nehemiah wrapped his arms around his mother's neck and hugged her tightly.

Just then, Zach came out of the bedroom yelling, "Mamma, mamma, I forgot to tell you. Mr. Smith came on the loudspeaker in my class and said that Nehemiah won, um, um...something," he said, trying to remember. Nehemiah told his mother about the selection of his essay in the Statewide Creative Writing Contest. "We won't know until Monday, who the winner will be," he said. He was hoping she wouldn't ask him what his essay was about. But she did.

"Oh, it was about birds," he said honestly. Seeming satisfied with his reply, she gave him a big hug. However, this time her hug didn't hinder his breathing.

"I guess blessings are being poured all over this family today," she declared proudly.

It was Friday, the last day of the school week. Everyone arrived to school on time and was quietly sitting down at their desks. Something was different. Nehemiah scanned the classroom. Nothing. But something definitely was different. He glanced across the rows of desk, until he happened to notice Mary Johnson shyly smiling. She was smiling like a person who wasn't quite sure how it should be done. Nehemiah quickly looked at something else, because he knew in a second, she would be rolling her eyes or sticking her tongue out at him. But for some reason, his eyes automatically gazed at her again. And she actually did it again! She was smiling at him! He turned his head so fast this time, that it made a swishing sound.

He rested his face on the palms of his hands and thought to himself, "Maybe something happened to the muscles in her face and now that strange smile is painted on like that forever!" Nehemiah chuckled at the thought. Mary's smile looked as if it was put on with crazy glue.

Mrs. Jones decided, after witnessing Mary's horrendous behavior the other day, that all of her students needed to understand the importance of learning how to fellowship with one another.

"Good morning class," Mrs. Jones said. "Today, we are going to change from our usual routine of classwork." Silence covered the room.

Mrs. Jones studied the class and continued, "I have decided to devote every Friday as the day that we will learn and practice an encouraging word." The silence continued. Mrs. Jones noticing all of the blank facial expressions decided to ask, "Who can tell me what fellowship means?" Some students indicated they didn't know either by hunching their shoulders, shaking their heads slowly from side to side, or some other non-verbal reply. Then all of a sudden, before he realized what he had done, Nehemiah's hand shot straight up in the air. Mrs. Jones was astonished. Nehemiah had never volunteered to give an answer in class before.

"Yes, Nehemiah," she asked enthusiastically. He knew the answer because he remembered one time when he was at church, the preacher told them to fellowship with each other and explained what it meant. Nehemiah could feel his classmates eyes on him. In a nervous voice that went from high to low, he answered, "Fellowship means friendship." Gaining confidence, he continued, "It means treating others the way you would like them to treat you." The students all eyed one another, but no one made a sound.

"Very good, Nehemiah. That's exactly what fellowship means," replied Mrs. Jones. Nehemiah saw John Greene and Mary Johnson staring as if they didn't recognize him. He smiled sheepishly. Deep down inside, something always told him that he wasn't dumb. "This has been the best week ever," he reflected. "Tuesday, Mr. Smith told me that my essay was selected to be in the contest and today I answered a question and didn't hear anyone call me a space cadet! What next?" he wondered.

Mrs. Jones continued with the lesson, "Fellowship is our word for today. Let's do a little brainstorming and see if we can come up with some interesting ideas relating to this word." Mary Johnson was the first person to raise her hand.

"Yes, Mary," Mrs. Jones stated.

"Uh, uh, I uh," Mary stumbled over her words. She even nibbled on the eraser of her pencil.

Mrs. Jones noticed a change in Mary ever since she told the class about the qualities of a truly smart person. Why just yesterday, she overheard Mary say 'excuse me' when she stepped on someone's foot. This morning, she actually saw her smiling sincerely at Nehemiah Peterson. And now, she was trying to share her ideas about fellowship and was having a difficult time expressing herself.

"Poor child," Mrs. Jones thought. "This is probably the first time in her life that she is trying to give a heartfelt response without looking for praise and applause. It's so obvious, she's hasn't played on a team unless she's the captain." Mrs. Jones analyzed, "But now the time has come for her to discover how to be a friend." Mrs. Jones momentarily felt a little sadness for Mary, because she looked like a dethroned queen.

"Mrs. Jones," Mary announced in an unfamiliar voice, "I would like to share something with the class about fellowship." Mrs. Jones nodded her head in Mary's direction. Mary walked to the front

of the classroom. After clearing her throat she began, "I uh...I just want to say that I'm sorry to everyone here." She even looked at Mrs. Jones who was sitting at her desk with her hands folded. "Mrs. Jones made me realize the other day that I'm not as smart as I thought I was. Everyone here knows that I have never helped anyone, but I made sure they helped me whenever I needed it. I have been unkind and selfish," Mary continued. "Last night, I had a dream that I had no place to live, nothing to eat and no one would help me. All of you passed by me and laughed. Then I said, 'I thought you were my friends.' And you answered, 'If we were your friends, why did you walk all over us and treat us like dirt?' Mary lowered her head shamefully and said, "I'm sorry".

Mrs. Jones watched as Mary humbly walked back to her seat. "The caterpillar has just turned into a butterfly," she said, taking a deep breath.

For the remainder of the day, the students wrote poems, invented games, solved puzzles, made pictures, and even put on a little skit. The laughter echoed throughout the room and Mrs. Jones joined in their merriment. When it was time for lunch, everyone remained in class and ate there. Mrs. Jones even played music and one by one everyone joined in, and began singing.

After the students were dismissed to go home, Mrs. Jones sat at her desk, satisfied that she had accomplished the first part of her goal. The students were on their way. Traveling the road of discovery, they would understand that together so much can be accomplished, if everyone extends a helping hand.

This was the best weekend that Nehemiah could ever remember. Things around his apartment had changed. His mother spent more time with them. She helped them with their homework. And she smiled more now. On Saturday, she surprised them with tickets to the circus. It had just come to town. They all thought the clowns were the funniest. Even their mother couldn't stop laughing at them. But the weekend went by quickly. In a flash, Saturday was gone and Sunday whizzed by.

It seemed as soon as their heads hit the pillow they heard, "It's Monday morning, boys. It's time to get up and get ready for school."

"Alright class," Mrs. Jones said. "I know you are all very anxious to find out who won the Statewide Creative Writing Contest."

Before she could continue, Mr. Smith came on the loudspeaker, "Good morning everyone at Garvey Elementary School." Nehemiah's heart was beating fast. It felt as if it had moved from the middle of his chest to his throat. He tried to swallow, but had a lump in his throat.

Mr. Smith continued with his announcement. "I know you've been waiting to find out who won the writing contest. You probably thought Monday was never going to get here," he laughed. John Greene hollered out, "Hurry up and get to the point!" Realizing too late where he was and what he had said, he put his hand across his mouth and slid down in his chair. The students laughed. Mrs. Jones didn't scold him. She just shook her finger at him, because she also wished that Mr. Smith would get to the point.

"Well," Mr. Smith dragged on. "The winner of the fourth-grade Statewide Creative Writing Contest is...Nehemiah Peterson." Everyone was jumping up and down, screaming and cheering. No one heard Mr. Smith congratulate Nehemiah over the loudspeaker. Nehemiah could hardly believe his ears. Mrs. Jones put her arms around him.

"I knew you could do it," she kept repeating. But he still couldn't believe it. Then their classroom door opened and Mr. Smith walked in smiling. He walked over to Nehemiah and shook his hand briskly. Mrs. Jones calmed the class down so that Mr. Smith could speak.

"Boys and girls, I know you are as happy as I am," he stated. He remembered the shocked faces they gave him last week, when he informed them that Nehemiah's essay had been selected to be in the contest. But today, the attitude in the class was not hostile.

Mr. Smith continued joyfully, "We are going to have an assembly tomorrow and the entire school will hear Nehemiah's paper. Not only that Nehemiah, but I am calling your mother to let her know that you won the contest and invite her to the assembly. Mr. Smith proceeded, "The Mayor of our town, Mayor Watson is going to present you with a certificate and a scholarship. Also, there will be photographers here from the local newspaper taking your picture."

Nehemiah waited hopefully, "I think he's really talking about me. I'm the Nehemiah Peterson who won the contest."

After Mr. Smith left the class, Nehemiah couldn't think of anything except, "Again, I have done something right."

He had a strong feeling this time that when Mr. Smith called his mother, informed her that he won the contest, and invited her to the assembly, she would say, "I'll be there." And this time, she would.

Nehemiah couldn't concentrate on school work for the rest of the day. His stomach made gurgling noises as it always did when he was excited. He was glad that they had a half-day of school. When he was leaving the school building, two sixth-grade boys who recognized him, walked up to him, slapped him five and said, "Right on, little brother."

Mrs. Perry saw him and gave him the thumbs up sign. Nehemiah felt like a thunderbolt had flown out of his body.

He and Zach ran all the way home. "Mamma! Mamma! I won the contest!" he said almost out of breath.

"I know," she said. "Mr. Smith called me on the phone and told me. He said the Mayor would be at the assembly tomorrow and they are going to put your picture in the newspaper! Oh, we are truly blessed!"

Nehemiah smiled at his mother. Now he knew for certain, that a blessing was something good. It changed families and made them better.

After everyone had eaten, Nehemiah, Zach and Sarah, sat in the living room and watched television. Their mother was putting away the left-over food. She was singing softly as she puttered about. Nehemiah listened as she sang. While he was listening to his mother singing, the mellow sound lulled him to sleep. His mother had to wake him up, tell him to get undressed and go to bed.

In bed that night, Nehemiah lay awake and thought about the assembly tomorrow. Zach wasn't asleep either. He got out of his bed, went over to Nehemiah and kissed him on the cheek.

"I'm proud that my brother is smart," he said. He turned around and went back to his bed.

Nehemiah knew he wouldn't be able to sleep tonight. He had never felt a sense of such total well-being in all his life. While lying in bed, he gazed out of the window. He could see thousands of stars in the sky and all of them were applauding him. Nehemiah closed his eyes tightly and made a wish on one of the stars that twinkled the brightest. Then he turned over and decided he'd better try to get some sleep, because he had a big day tomorrow.

The next morning, Nehemiah awoke to the whispering sound of his mother's voice bending over his bed, telling him it's time to get up. Zach was already up and dressed. Nehemiah saw that his mother had laid out his navy blue suit. The one he wore when he went to church. After he finished dressing, his mother asked him to bring her his black shoes.

She looked at the shoes that he handed her and said, "Look at these scuff marks on these shoes. You can't wear them like this. Go get me the grease and

an old cloth." She polished the shoes so well, that they looked like a brand new pair.

After he and Zach had finished their oatmeal and headed toward the door to leave for school, Nehemiah's mother said, "I'll see you boys at the assembly today."

Nehemiah smiled and said to himself, "I knew it! I knew it!"

When Nehemiah and Zach arrived at school, his class had already gone inside the building. He rushed into his classroom. Everyone was dressed as if they were going to a birthday party. Even Mrs. Jones had her hair fixed differently. When he closed the door, everyone began clapping. Nehemiah blushed and looked around the room.

He noticed that the room was decorated with balloons and there was a large sign that read, "Congratulations, Nehemiah, we all love you." Nehemiah saw that the two reading tables in the back of the room were covered with red and white tablecloths. There was a large cake in the middle of one of the tables.

Nehemiah slowly walked over to his desk and sat down. He was so overjoyed, that he thought he was going to cry. Everyone was still clapping, even John Greene and Mary Johnson. Mrs. Jones held her hand up to let everyone know that she was about to say something and the clapping diminished. The children quietly took their seats.

Mrs. Jones said, "In a few minutes, we will be going to the auditorium for the assembly. Our class will sit in the first two rows. When the assembly is over, we will all come back here for a party honoring Nehemiah." When Mrs. Jones finished speaking, she asked Nehemiah if he had anything he would like to say to the class. He hesitated. Then sluggishly he moved his legs to the side of his chair and stood up.

"Well," he said. "I'm glad that I won the contest. I hope everyone will enjoy my essay when I read it today. I'd like to say thank you for giving me a birthday party."

Everyone laughed and said, "BIRTHDAY PARTY?" However, this time Nehemiah laughed too. He knew that the children weren't laughing to be mean. He quickly corrected himself.

John yelled out, "That's okay Nehemiah, everyone makes mistakes sometimes. That's why they have erasers on pencils, to help us fix our mistakes." Agreement could be heard throughout the classroom.

Mrs. Jones asked everyone to line up at the door.

Mary, who was usually first in line, said, "Nehemiah, I think you should be at the head of the line today." Nehemiah stared at her in disbelief. But he looked in her eyes and they were smiling at him.

He said, "Thank you," as he took his position as the class leader.

When they arrived in the auditorium, the other classes were already seated. The first two rows had been left empty for their class. Nehemiah took his seat in the front row. He looked around to see if his mother was there, but he did not see her. He began to feel disappointed. However, when he turned to the entrance door of the auditorium, he saw his mother and baby sister Sarah come in behind Mr.

Smith. He noticed that there were other people following them.

Two of the men had cameras around their neck and small signs on their jackets that read, "The Press."

Mr. Smith ushered everyone that was following him up on stage. Nehemiah was so happy to see his mother and sister, that he sat up straight in his chair and held his head high as if he were a king sitting on his throne.

He heard a loud, familiar voice in the background yelling,"Hi, mamma." He turned around and saw that it was his brother Zach standing up by his class waving in the direction of his mother. There was a burst of laughter from the crowd. Then it settled down without anyone having to tell them to be quiet.

Mr. Smith began to speak into the microphone. "Testing, testing," he said. "Today, we have gathered together to honor a member of our school family, Nehemiah Peterson." There were enthusiastic cheers from the audience. Mr. Smith continued, "I'd like you to meet my guests who have also come to salute Nehemiah."

He introduced Mayor Watson, Mrs. Kendle, President of the school board, Mrs. Peterson, Nehemiah's mother, and his sister Sarah. He also introduced the two men with the cameras. He said that they were from the local newspaper. Mr. Smith asked Nehemiah to come up on the stage. Everyone clapped. The clapping carried him to the stage effortlessly.

you wrote for the contest. Would you please honor us by reading it?"

Nehemiah took the essay and approached the microphone shyly. The audience became still.

He cleared his throat and began, "If I could be anything in the world, I'd like to be a bird." When he finished reading the essay, the crowd was silent. Then all of a sudden, it was as if trumpets had sounded. Everyone was on their feet applauding feverishly. Nehemiah turned around anxiously searching for his mother's face. She was standing with tears proudly flowing down her face, drenching her smile.

When the crowd settled down, Mr. Smith moved towards the microphone and commented, "I have never heard anyone speak of nature with such love and admiration. I'm so overcome with jubilance, I don't think I can continue right now, so I'm going to let Mayor Watson take the microphone."

Mayor Watson was a big, robust man. He stood over six feet three inches tall. When he started speaking, his voice was deep and heavy. The walls and the floor in the auditorium vibrated when he spoke. He shook Nehemiah's hand and presented him with a savings bond to be used toward his college education, a $500.00 check, and a certificate that read, STATEWIDE CREATIVE WRITING CONTEST WINNER...NEHEMIAH PETERSON. The crowd clapped, whistled, and threw pencils in the air. The men from the press took a picture of Nehemiah standing beside Mayor Watson, Mr. Smith, Mrs. Kendle, and his mother and sister. Even Zach came on stage to get into the picture. Nehemiah that read, STATEWIDE CREATIVE WRITING CON-TEST WINNER...NEHEMIAH PETERSON. The crowd clapped, whistled, and threw pencils in the air. The men from the press took a picture of Nehemiah standing beside Mayor Watson, Mr. Smith, Mrs. Kendle, and his mother and sister. Even Zach came on stage to get into the picture. Nehemiah held the savings bond in front of him so that the photographers could get a picture of it and his mother held the check.

After they finished taking pictures, Nehemiah confidently approached the microphone for a second time. When he grabbed it this time, he was sure of himself and knew exactly what he was going to say.

"Boys and girls," he announced. "I'd like to tell you something. Most of my life, I didn't think that I could do anything right. My assignments were always wrong, even though I really tried hard. All the other students in my class had things they did well, but I couldn't do anything. All I ever did well was daydream and I got yelled at in class for doing that." He continued, "When Mrs. Jones told us we had to write an essay for the contest and to daydream before we started writing. I didn't have any trouble. I knew I was going to write about my world; a place where I fit in and if I made a mistake, no one paid attention to it. I'm very happy that I won the contest and would like to be a writer when I grow up. I want to be a good student and always be a blessing to my family. I finally realize that I've always had something important to say. Also, I want everyone here today to know that I'M SPE-

CIAL, TOO! I'M SPECIAL, TOO! And each and every one of you are special. My teacher, Mrs. Jones told our class never to look down at anyone, unless you are helping them up. And she was right. People fear other people who are different from themselves. I'm not talking about the kind of fear where you cover up and hide your head under a blanket. I'm talking about the kind of fear that makes you avoid someone because he or she doesn't read or spell as well as you or doesn't have clothes as nice as yours." He continued, "If you have this attitude, then you should do something about it right away. As Mrs. Jones said, you never know when you might need help."

The audience went wild with their cheers.

When they quieted down again, Nehemiah continued, "All of us have some special talents that are hidden within us. When you begin to have faith and believe in yourself, the light inside of you will shine brightly on the outside, for everyone to see."

The captivated crowd stared at Nehemiah while he was speaking. He didn't know it then, but his inner light was shining and was felt by everyone there.

Nehemiah continued in a strong and confident voice, "If you don't look for it, it will remain hidden forever. You can be anything you want to be in the world, if you do your very best and never give up. Anything is possible and it doesn't matter where you come from, where you live or the color of your skin."

LESSON ACTIVITY:

THINK   WRITE   REVISE   IMPLEMENT

1. Make a list of things that are important to you and give a complete explanation why they are important.

2. What is self-esteem? What affects your self-esteem? Do you suffer from low self-esteem? What are some causes of low self-esteem? What must you do in order to build positive self-esteem?

3. What are goals? Why is it important to set them? What goal (s) have you set for yourself? How do you plan on accomplishing them and what timetable have you set for yourself.

LESSON ACTIVITY - (DEFINITIONS):

DIRECTIONS: Review the list of words and write the correct word next to the matching definition on the line provided.

1. Value	6. Self-esteem
2. Forgiveness	7. Blame
3. Acceptance	8. Self-image
4. Unique	9. Motivation
5. Goals	10.Responsible

_ belief in oneself   _____

_ to stimulate into action   _____

_ to find fault with   _____

_ a person's concept of him/herself   _____

_ the purpose that one works to fulfill   _____

_ to give up resentment   _____

_ to be accountable for one's behavior   _____

_ special; one of a kind   _____

_ being respected for who you are   _____

_ a principle or standard   _____

LESSON ACTIVITY

1. Which characters in the story learned how to change their negative qualities and develop positive ones?

2. How did Nehemiah recognize that his differences were not weaknesses, but strengths? Explain.

3. How can each of us be alike, yet have special qualities that make us different? Explain.

4. How did Nehemiah feel about himself after he won the contest?

5. Explain what is meant by the sentence, "Mary Johnson looked like a dethroned queen?"

6. Do you believe that parents always know the correct things to do? Explain your answer by giving examples.

7. What are some of the problems that resulted in low-self esteem for Nehemiah and his mother. How were these problems solved? Explain.

8. Can a person who boasts about their achievements have a self-esteem problem? Explain.

9. What is faith and how does it affect one's self-esteem and self-image?

10. What did Mrs. Jones mean when she said, "The caterpillar has become a butterfly?" Explain.